BARRIO STREETS
CARNIVAL DREAMS

Three Generations
of Latino Artistry

EDITED BY

LORI MARIE
CARLSON

HENRY HOLT AND COMPANY
NEW YORK

Henry Holt and Company, Inc.
Publishers since 1866
115 West 18th Street
New York, New York 10011

Henry Holt is a registered
trademark of Henry Holt and Company, Inc.

Published in Canada by Fitzhenry & Whiteside Ltd.,
195 Allstate Parkway, Markham, Ontario L3R 4T8.

Library of Congress Cataloging-in-Publication Data
Barrio streets carnival dreams: three generations of Latino artistry / edited by Lori Marie Carlson.
        p.   cm.—(Edge Books)
    Summary: A collection of Latino literature, poetry, artwork, and commentary celebrating the
contributions of three generations of twentieth-century Americans of Mexican, Caribbean, and
South American descent.
    1. Children's literature, American—Hispanic American authors. 2. Hispanic Americans—
Literary collections. 3. Hispanic Americans—Juvenile literature. 4. Hispanic Americans in art.
[1. Hispanic Americans—Literary collections. 2. American literature—Hispanic American
authors—Collections. 3. Hispanic Americans in art.]
    I. Carlson, Lori M.   II. Series.   PZ5.B27   1996   [Fic]—dc20   95-41317

ISBN 0-8050-4120-6

First Edition—1996

Printed in the United States of America on acid-free paper. ∞
10   9   8   7   6   5   4   3   2   1

for my sister,
Leigh Ann,
whose gifts are from the heart, *siempre*

CONTENTS

INTRODUCTION

LORI MARIE CARLSON

People often ask me how my interest and career in Latin American and Latino literature and culture originated. Do I have Spanish-speaking parents? Did I grow up in a Latin American country? The answer is no; however, my heritage did shape my future. Looking back on my childhood, I realize that my mother's Italian ancestry added zest and a tiny bit of defiance to my father's more quiet Swedish heritage. It is probably the rub of my parents' cultures that pushed me toward my career.

In Jamestown, New York, my hometown, the predominant ethnic and religious influences were Northern European and Protestant, and these weighed upon my mother's awareness of her ethnicity. For her, being Italian American wasn't always easy. In subtle and more direct ways she let me know that she had experienced prejudice. And on the national level, there were far more symbolic examples. Had I realized, she once asked me, that none of our presidents had ever been Italian? She usually would talk about such matters while cooking something delicious in the kitchen—something garlicky and pungent with basil and rosemary. And I would think about her feelings and her well-camouflaged hurt and wonder just why this was, considering how exceptional—at least in my opinion—were the contributions of Italians to the world (not least of all in cuisine). She told me more and more about bias and injustice, and I started thinking that my sister and I were lucky to have our father's very Swedish surname.

While I felt no more loyalty to one ancestry than to the other, I did begin to harbor a secret joy that I was, in some way, also a minority. Well, maybe not a minority but certainly not a Yankee. I am fond of underdogs and I began to feel like one. What made my little secret even more fun was the fact that no one ever suspected that my blond hair and light blue eyes hid the darker, more brunette traits of my mom.

When I was old enough to start reading the local newspaper, I realized that few ethnic-sounding names were mentioned in positive stories. It was then that I decided to do something—I hadn't yet decided what—for those who had to live with prejudice. It was the age of activism. And as a young teen in the early '70s I was interested in the social and racial issues facing our nation at that time.

I was thirteen when I befriended a girl whose family had just come from Puerto Rico to our town of maple trees and blizzardy winters. And our friendship, formed in seventh-grade Spanish class at Jefferson Jr. High, led me to a fascination with her traditions. I discovered that being able to speak another language did important things for me: It kept me close in some mysterious way to my mother's ancestry and it fired my imagination. Speaking Spanish just might allow me to create another kind of life outside of my hometown; a life of travel and exciting places, interesting situations and progressive ideas. I had Technicolor visions of a future in which a mature version of myself socialized with diplomats, artists, scholars, led a life of independence, all the while communicating in this magic tongue.

That vision did become my life. After years of university study in Hispanic literature, I took my credentials to New York City and started working with the same Latin American and Latino authors I had read in graduate school. I met painters of renown, befriended diplomats, and even had my hand kissed by the president of Argentina! That I have been so fortunate, so touched with bounty by the Spanish language and the cultures of our southern neighbors, is a blessing that I want to share.

This book is a tribute to the myriad individuals and traditions that give meaning to the heritage that is Hispanic or Latino. (Both terms refer to Americans of Latin American ancestry, but, depending on perspective, culture, and age, one may be preferable to the other.) Beautiful and ancient traditions, inclinations, and beliefs endow Latino culture with its bold and unusual power. Yes, *power,* because more than any other ethnic group in this country, Latinos have drawn attention to the issue of whether or not one should keep one's language of origin, and they have fought to keep their values—familial, social, and religious—intact.

Why is this? I believe the answers can be found in geography and history. We share two linked continents; together we are the "New World." Then, too, before the 1848 Treaty of Guadalupe Hidalgo ended the Mexican-American War, Mexico governed the vast lands now known as Texas, California, most of Arizona and New Mexico, and parts of Colorado, Utah, and Nevada. Spanish roots run very, very deep in North American soil. We need to look back to those earlier days in order to look ahead to our shared future.

Barrio Streets Carnival Dreams can be read as several books in one. All three sections contain poetry, storytelling, cuisine, music, spirituality, and graphic design. But the selections within each reflect the tastes and experiences of a particular historical moment. Each section is independent yet, in interesting ways, mirrors the others. *Barrio Streets Carnival Dreams* celebrates the contributions that three generations of twentieth-century Americans of Mexican, Caribbean, and South American roots have made to our country, as well as the gifts that current artists of the same heritage are passing on to Americans of the next century. Some of the personalities will be familiar and others, I hope, wonderful new inspirations. This book is not a complete guide to Hispanic cultural traditions. Instead it offers a palette of suggestions that hint at the rich heritage of the many Americans whose ancestry can be rightly defined as Hispanic. This collection of insights, secrets, songs, and evocations is my way of saying *"gracias, mil veces"* to all of those who have shared their stories and their gifts with me.

INSTALLATION "KINGDOM,"
COPYRIGHT © 1996 BY JOSÉ LUIS ORTIZ
10′ X 10′ WOODCUT

■ ■ ■

BELLO ESPAÑOL

MAGDALENA HIJUELOS

Translated from the Spanish

by Lori M. Carlson

Magdalena Hijuelos came to the United States from Cuba before the Second World War. For more than forty years she has lived in New York City, where she loves to explore the city's neighborhoods, meet people, attend mass, and write poetry.

BELLO ESPAÑOL
Quiero dedicarle
una balada de amor
a mi bello español
tan sencillo
que se deja arrastrar
como la brisa del mar

BEAUTIFUL SPANISH
I want to dedicate
a love song
to my beautiful Spanish language
so natural
it flows
as a breeze from the sea

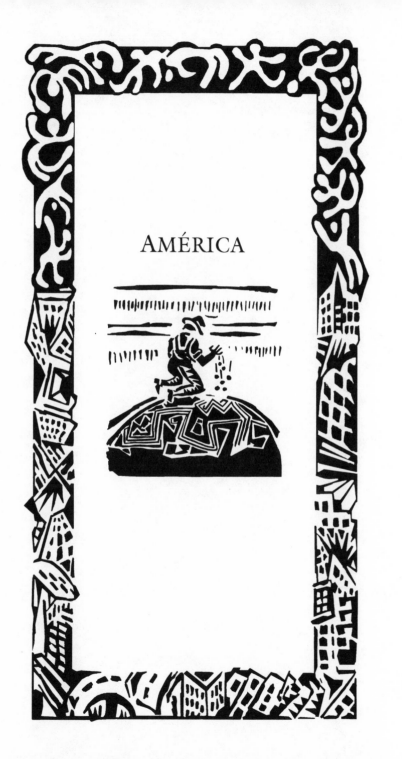

AMÉRICA

Long before the founding of the United States, Spaniards, Indians, and Mexicans, infused the land with a sensibility and a vision totally their own. In the nineteenth and early twentieth centuries, Mexicans and Spaniards in the Southwest and West, and Spaniards, Puerto Ricans, and Cubans in the East helped to shape the growing nation. But these "Spanish American" populations, which shared a common language, religion, and folklore, existed as fairly isolated communities in North America. Spanish-speaking Americans were usually thought of as immigrants in little pools dispersed here and there throughout the "colossus." Although Cubans and Puerto Ricans had been coming to New York since before the turn of the century, many more would follow after the 1898 Treaty of Paris granted Cuba independence from Spain and ceded Puerto Rico to the United States. And waves of Mexicans came to find work in the border territory comprised of Texas, New Mexico, Arizona, California, and Colorado.

A small tin-frame mirror reflecting an artistic practice dating back to the turn of the century . . . a portrait of two curious birds . . . Carnival and Afro-Cuban music . . . In the first part of *Barrio Streets Carnival Dreams,* painters, poets, musicians, and artists who have had a lasting influence inspire us to remember that our lives resonate with the love, vision, and work of our *antepasados.*

✖ ✖ ✖

HOJALATERÍA

When the Santa Fe Trail opened trade with northern Mexico in the early nineteenth century, merchants and traders followed. Soon new products were flowing westward to be sold to Hispanic settlers. After the Mexican-American War, when the territory became part of the United States under the name of New Mexico, many more goods were transported along the trail. Fats and oils arrived in tin boxes, and this tin was later put to good use by Hispanic tinsmiths, known as hojalateros. *These* hojalateros *made functional yet stylish objects for their churches and homes: candlestick holders, frames for religious and secular paintings, crosses, small boxes decorated with bits of glass, among other items. Their tinwares are known as* hojalatería. *The tin-framed mirror depicted here was given to me by a friend.*

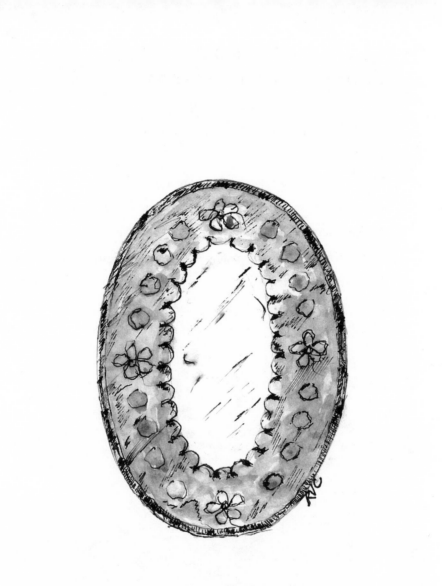

DRAWING OF A TIN FRAME MIRROR,
AN EXAMPLE OF *HOJALATERÍA*.

❉ ❉ ❉
EL DESCUBRIMIENTO DE LA GRAN MANHATITLÁN

FELIPE GALINDO-FEGGO

Felipe Galindo, whose cartoons are signed by his pen name Feggo, is a free-lance cartoonist and illustrator. His cartoons regularly appear in The New York Times *and other publications; among his books are* Cats Will Be Cats.

El Descubrimiento de la gran Manhattitlán

⬛ ⬛ ⬛

TRISTE MIRADA

FELIPE ALFAU

Translated from the Spanish

by Ilan Stavans

Some of the most beautiful lyric poetry in the world is written in Spain and Latin America. Lyricism in language describes feelings, moods, and impressions rather than ideas or events. Whether inspired by spiritual yearning or romantic feeling, lyric poetry flows like music. Poetry in Spanish often has that musical, magical quality. Here, for example, is a poem by the late Spanish American novelist and poet Felipe Alfau, who came to the United States from Spain in 1916 when he was just fourteen. Although Mr. Alfau wrote his novels in English, he chose to write poetry in his native Spanish because he believed "poetry is too close to the heart."

TRISTE MIRADA

Triste mirada;
si así te torna el invierno sombrío,
no dejes que la helada
te envuelva en el sudario de su frío,
triste mirada. No pienses en la nieve
ni que desde el otoño, desde el estío,
llueve . . . llueve . . .
No te des al hastío,
triste mirada. Anímate y no llores
Si miras hacia afuera,
verás que llueve, sí; pero es que llueven flores.
¿No ves que ya está aquí la primavera?

SAD EYES

Sad eyes;
that's what the somber winter makes you,
don't allow the frost to
envelop you in a shroud of coldness,
sad eyes. Don't think of the snow,
of the rain falling since autumn, since summer.
The rain!
Don't give in to boredom,
sad eyes. Cheer up and don't cry!
If you look out you'll see
that, indeed, it's raining. But it's raining flowers!
Spring is here. Can't you see?

⚎ ⚎ ⚎

EXCERPT FROM
THE STORY OF DESI ARNAZ
AND HIS BAND: ROADS
WITHIN A CUBAN HEART

MARCO RIZO

Marco Rizo and Desi Arnaz were boyhood friends in Santiago, Cuba, long before they collaborated as musicians on the I Love Lucy *show. Among the feelings they shared while growing up was a deep appreciation for the African culture in their land. African rhythm and dance influenced their musicality in energetic, new ways. In the following excerpt from Mr. Rizo's autobiographical work,* The Story of Desi Arnaz and His Band: Roads Within a Cuban Heart, *the tradition of the Carnival procession as experienced by the two boys in their hometown comes alive.*

I recall one Saturday evening, toward the end of a warm July, Carnival festivities had already run for several weekends, and that particular night was the culmination of three days of celebration: Santa Cristina, Santiago, and Santa Ana. My parents had left me in the care of my mother's sister, Caridad Ayala, affectionately known to us as "Tía Cary."

Aunt Cary was a liberal-natured woman who allowed me more freedom than my parents would have ever permitted. She let me *look* at the carnival! The event of unbridled revelry could be compared to late-night TV with scenes parents don't want their children to watch.

I stood alongside her as we peered from the balcony of our second-story home, and suddenly it sounded as though a riot was coming down the street. As the source of the commotion approached, we saw a horseman dressed in white, leading what appeared to be a mob engaged in a riot. The rider played Oriental-sounding music on a trumpetlike instrument.

"Marco, that's called a Chinese cornet," remarked Aunt Cary. It sounded more like an oboe to me.

The horseman's song was answered with an explosion of sound, for a marching band followed closely behind. This exchange seemed to represent a musical dialogue that was repeated over and over again, growing louder and louder as the parade approached, and fading as it disappeared from view.

Suddenly, the atmosphere was charged again by another string of paraders banging on frying pans, shaking maracas, and scraping gourds. Conga drums were pounded, and the rhythmic clacking of claves set the pace for the off-beat procession. Rattles of wood, boxes, spoons, and toys comprised the band, and participants sported wild colors and costumes, masks and hats, while singing and gyrating to the rhythm of the conga. This is the *comparsa,* the typical parade procession of Cuban Carnival.

Each *comparsa* was a miniature description of an era of Cuban history and music. They bore unique names derived from their neighborhood or *cabildo:* "*Los Hoyos,*" "*El Tivoli,*" "*Los Alacránes.*" One of the paraders held a huge scorpion mask over his head as others closely following held up the tail. Another dancer carried a *farola,* a tall decorated pole lit with candles. The smells of sweat, tobacco, and liquor pervaded the air.

Aunt Cary singled out costumes and characteristics of the participants: French Creole, African, native Cuban Indian, Spanish, mulatto, English, and Chinese. Spain, Africa, Italy, England, France, Portugal, and the Orient have all made generous contributions to this musical and visual mosaic. Santiago Carnivals must have been the most diverse in the world!

A *charanga,* a Cuban ragtime band, with flute, violins, clarinet, trombone, horns, bass, drums, and native percussion instruments, set up on a street corner directly in front of us. They began to play a *contradanza,* a country dance, and Afro-Cubans dressed in white re-created the choreography of this English-origin dance imported from Haiti.

Some of the revelers stopped and entered homes, putting on a show for their hosts. At Carnival time, class distinctions were thrown out, and everyone felt free to barge in, play music and dance, drink, and help themselves to whatever they could find in your house. Those without instruments joined in the music making by beating rhythms on tabletops, wooden boxes, pots, or tin cans. After a few minutes the group takes off to have fun somewhere else.

Comparsas were often comprised of Afro-Cubans who dyed their hair a bright scarlet and painted their faces a soft light color. Others painted themselves as blacks, using vermilion on their lips and white on their eyebrows. Mulattoes painted their cheeks bright red, and wore fake beards and yellow wigs made of tinted leaves. Their costumes consisted of everyday clothes turned inside out, embellished with shiny cords of brass or copper to give the appearance of gold and silver. Others paraded with their faces painted black, red, and bronze, wearing a man's hat and a woman's long, low-cut robe with short sleeves.

It was not unusual to see men dressed as women, though the reverse was never seen. We often heard stories of how the masquerade resulted in confusion or even embarrassment. One young man, after having blurred his eyes with a few drinks, made a pass at a young woman. When he got close enough to see the black stubble all over her face, he realized she was a man and beat a hasty retreat.

I had just about had enough of this revelry when a passing *comparsa* caught my eye. Two very white hands were frantically waving at us. The masked face gave no clue as to who they belonged to until the parader shouted up at our window in a small falsetto voice:

"¡Hola, Marco! ¿Me conoces? ["Hi, Marco! Do you recognize me?"]

"Desi, is that you?"

"Sí, Marco. How on earth could you tell that it's me? Why aren't you down here with us? What's wrong with you? Are you dead? You don't know what you're missing!"

Within moments he was swept away with the parade. A few minutes later, he was alongside me, pulling me down the stairs before Aunt Cary could say no.

He threw me a set of claves he had had in his back pocket, and he continued to bang wildly on his *boku,* the small conga that later brought him fame and fortune.

The conga rhythm, with its relentless, irresistible drive, works like magic on listeners. It is impossible to maintain control of your feet and body. As the energy of this music spreads to crowds of thousands of onlookers standing by, everyone begins to dance. For Desi and me, this was pure fun. We never dreamed that this might be training for a future job.

As our *comparsa* snaked through Santiago's streets, we stopped and observed an authentic Cuban rumba or *güagüancó.* This dance is different from the popular North American ballroom dance, but, nonetheless, it does contain some of the same elements. It is a sexy dance, rooted in the barnyard mating ritual of the rooster and the chicken, much like the *cueca* of Chile.

The dance, more typical of Havana than Santiago, had by this time achieved notoriety throughout the island. A small group of percussionists provided the music for the show. The male dancer wore a shirt with ruffled sleeves; his partner wore a dress with a long ruffled tail and waved

15

a handkerchief in her hand. The dancers moved within two or three feet of each other as they jumped and spun. The woman lifted her dress to tease and to beckon her partner to come closer, gyrating her hips like a hula dancer. The male dancer got really warmed up, and he violently threw himself at his partner. She moved back to avoid contact with him. If ratings could be applied to dances, as they are to movies, I suppose it would be a PG-13.

As we grew, our culture became an object of fascination, and we failed to understand the reasoning that drove the prejudices against the African-derived culture of our neighbors. Desi was moved even more deeply—he heard the call of the wild from deep within—a call to solidarity with his African compatriots that cut across artificially imposed social barriers. It was inconceivable to Desi to be his neighbor's enemy after dancing the conga with him. On the surface, at least, Carnival music seemed to offer love, joy, and unity, ideals which all of humanity naturally longed for.

✠ ✠ ✠

MAXIMS BY JOSÉ MARTÍ

Translated from the Spanish

by Lori M. Carlson

José Martí, the great Cuban poet, lived in New York City from January 3, 1880 until shortly before his death on May 19, 1895. While in New York he founded a children's magazine entitled La Edad de Oro *(The Golden Age). Throughout his life he fought for freedom, particularly for his beloved Cuba. Although Martí wrote a lot of poetry and essays, he is probably known best in the United States for the lyrics of the song "Guantanamera," which begin with the beautiful lines* "Yo soy un hombre sincero/De donde crece la palma" (I am a sincere man/From a place where the palms grow). *Martí also wrote many philosophical sayings as a way to instruct and encourage his fellow countrymen.*

Sólo hay una puerta para la libertad, y es el trabajo.
There is only one door to freedom, and it is work.

Ser bueno es el único modo de ser dichoso. Ser culto, es el único modo de ser libre.
To be good is the only way to be happy. To be educated, is the only way to be free.

Las manos de los poetas cierran siempre las heridas que abre la ira de los hombres.
The hands of poets always heal the wounds caused by mankind's anger.

Las batallas se ganan entre ceja y ceja.
Battles are won between the eyebrows.

Los libros consuelan, calman, preparan, enriquecen y redimen.
Books comfort, calm, prepare, enrich and redeem.

THE PARROT WHO WOULDN'T SAY "CATAÑO"

PURA BELPRÉ

When young Pura Belpré came to New York City in 1921 she thought that she would only attend her sister's wedding and then go home to Puerto Rico. But she liked Manhattan so much that she decided to stay. She eventually became the first Hispanic librarian in the New York Public Library system. Her special way of telling stories made her well known throughout the United States. Soon adults liked to listen to her folktales just as much as children. In her introduction to one of her story collections, The Tiger and the Rabbit and Other Tales, *she had this to say about the tradition of telling tales:*

Growing up on the island of Puerto Rico in an atmosphere of natural storytellers was fun: a father whose occupation took him all over the island; a grandmother whose stories always ended with a nonsense rhyme or song, setting feet to jump, skip or dance; elder sisters who still remembered tales told by my mother; and finally, a stepmother whose literary taste was universal.

No one ever went to bed without a round of stories told. The characters of the favorite ones soon became part of an everyday life: one traveled to strange lands of shepherds, princesses and princes, Kings and Queens; laughed at the cunning of animals and suffered with the punished ones; and waited expectantly for the mysterious appearance of the three Magi.

Where did the stories come from?

They came from a cultural background of all the people who centuries back discovered and ruled the country. They are part of a folklore verbally preserved and enriched by the creative power of a people who, drawing from the hills, mountains, cities, and valleys, produced the folklore of Puerto Rico.

Across the bay from San Juan in Puerto Rico is a town called Cataño. Here, long ago, lived a retired sailor called Yuba. His only possession and sole companion was a parrot—a beautiful, talkative bird known to all the town. Much as the parrot talked, there was one thing she refused to say. That was the name of the town. No matter how hard Yuba tried to teach her, she would never say the word. This saddened Yuba who loved his town very much.

"You are an ungrateful bird," Yuba told the parrot. "You repeat everything you hear, yet refuse to say the name of the town where you have lived most of your life." But all the parrot would do was to blink her beady eyes and talk of other things.

One day as Yuba sat on his balcony with the parrot on his knee, arguing as usual, who should come by but Don Casimiro, the rich poultry fancier from San Juan. He stopped and listened. In all his years he had never heard such a parrot. What a wonderful addition to his poultry yard she would make! The more he listened to her conversation, the more he wanted to own her.

"Would you sell me that parrot?" he said at last. "I will pay you well for her."

"Neither silver nor gold can buy her, Señor," said Yuba.

Don Casimiro was surprised. To all appearances this man looked as if he could use some money. "What else would you take for her, my good man?" he asked.

"Nothing. But I will make a bargain with you," replied Yuba.

"A bargain? What kind of a bargain?" Don Casimiro wanted to know.

"I have been trying to teach her to say 'Cataño,' But for reasons of her own she refuses to say it. Well, take her with you. If you can make her say it, the bird is yours and I will be grateful to you for the rest of my life. If you fail, bring her back to me."

"Agreed," said Don Casimiro delightedly. He took the parrot, thanked Yuba, and left.

Late that afternoon he returned home. He sat in the spacious corridor facing the courtyard filled with fancy fowls and potted plants. "Now," he said to the parrot, "repeat after me: *Ca-ta-ño!*" And he took great care to say each syllable clearly and slowly. The parrot flapped her wings, but said not a word.

"Come, come," said Don Casimiro. "Say *Ca-ta-ño*." The parrot blinked her beady eyes at him, but said not a word.

"But you can say anything you want. I have heard you speak. Let's try it again. *Ca-ta-ño*." Don Casimiro waited, but the parrot sauntered down the corridor as if she were deaf.

Now Don Casimiro was a man of great wealth but little patience. His temper was as hot as the chili peppers he grew in his vegetable patch. He strode after the parrot who had stopped beside a large potted fern at the end of the corridor. He grabbed the bird and shook her. "Say *CA-TA-ÑO!*" he commanded through clenched teeth.

The parrot blinked and quickly wriggled herself out of his hands. But Don Casimiro picked her up again and held her fast. "Say *Ca-ta-ño,* or I will wring your neck and throw you out of the window!"

The parrot said not a word.

Blinded with anger, Don Casimiro hurled her out of the window, forgetting to wring her neck. The parrot landed in the chicken coop.

That night a strange noise rose from the courtyard. Don Casimiro awoke with a start. "Thieves!" he cried.

Thinking they were after his fowls he rushed out of the house and headed for the chicken coop. What a turmoil! Chicken feathers flew every which way. Pails of water and chicken feed were overturned. Squawking chickens ran hither and thither; others lay flat on the ground as though they were dead.

Suddenly, from the far end of the coop rose a voice

saying: "Say *Ca-ta-ño,* or I will wring your neck and throw you out of the window!"

There, perched on a rafter, was the parrot, clutching one of the most precious fowls. Don Casimiro rushed to the spot and pulled the parrot down.

Before the sun had risen he was aboard the ferry boat on the way to Yuba's home. The parrot sat on his knees as if she had forgotten the happenings of the night before. He found Yuba sitting on his balcony sipping a cup of black coffee.

"So you failed too," said Yuba sadly.

"Oh, no, no!" Don Casimiro replied. "She said 'Cataño' all right! But the bargain is off. I want you to take her back."

Yuba was puzzled.

Don Casimiro noticed his confusion and quickly added: "You see, she played havoc in my chicken house before she said 'Cataño.' "

Yuba's face shone with happiness. He took the parrot and held her close. He watched Don Casimiro hurrying down the street toward the ferry boat station.

"Say *Ca-ta-ño,*" he whispered to the parrot.

"Cataño, Cataño," the parrot replied.

And since that day no one was happier, in all of Cataño, than Yuba the retired sailor.

BLACK-CAPPED MOCKING THRUSH

LOUIS AGASSIZ FUERTES

Many experts believe ornithologist Louis Agassiz Fuertes to be America's greatest painter of birds. Puerto Rican by his father's heritage, he was born in 1874 in Ithaca, New York, and died in 1927. For many years he worked for the American Museum of Natural History in New York City. The bird mates he has painted here are a pair of Black-capped Mocking Thrushes (Donacobius atricapillus).

PAINTING OF BLACK-CAPPED MOCKING THRUSH,
KNOWN AS *DONACOBIUS ATRICAPILLUS*.

⁜ ⁜ ⁜

LILIES AND FRIJOLES

SUSAN LOWELL

Susan Lowell was born in Chihuahua City, Chihuahua, Mexico, and has lived on both sides of the Mexican-American border. She is a fourth-generation Arizonan, descended from ranchers, gold miners, explorers, artists, and schoolteachers. The author of the novella Ganado Red, *she is also a successful children's book writer.*

On the last day of May, my grandmother's lilies have begun to bloom. Last week I cut the stalk in bud, submerging the thick slimy stem in a blue vase on my desk, where I could watch the lilies as they opened—if they only would, for I was afraid I'd picked them too soon. But they did. And as they bloom, one by one, like surprising new gifts from the land of the dead, they make me sit here and remember, remember . . .

My grandmother's garden surrounded the small house where she, a widow, lived alone, and her garden was surrounded in turn by cattle ranches and cotton fields and miles and miles of Arizona desert. The whole landscape was dominated by the mountain to the north, a huge raw rock called *Picacho* in Spanish, and, quite redundantly,

Picacho Peak in English. My grandmother spoke both languages. "*¡Ay, Chihuahua mi tierra caramba!*" she used to exclaim in amazement. I especially liked that mild oath because Chihuahua was literally *mi tierra;* I was born there. Spanish and English were two of my grandmother's treasures, along with her little ranch, her collection of cream pitchers from around the world, her shotgun, her flowers, her shelf of curious old books inherited from her Scottish Canadian father, her tough mind and body, her affectionate heart, her recipe for *frijoles,* and her stories.

She was born Lavina Cumming, in the town of Nogales, Arizona, just a few hundred yards from Nogales, Sonora, in the year 1893, when Arizona was a territory, Sonora was a state, and the border between the two was considerably more fluid than it is today. People were born on one side of the line or the other, yet they more or less lived where they chose, moving back and forth for reasons of convenience, business, pleasure, or sometimes political necessity, as in the cases of the Apache bands pursued by the U.S. cavalry, and the Yaqui Indians chased by the Mexican army.

"Do you want to hear a true story . . . or one of that *other* kind?" my grandmother used to ask.

My brothers and I knew what was expected of us: "Oh, a true story, Grandmama, please."

The true stories were short, some only a few words long, and they were always memorable: "One night, when we lived in Peru, a vampire bat bit me in the throat. Here, you can touch the place."

Her throat was brown, fat, and soft, and it smelled of Revlon face powder. There were no visible vampire toothmarks, but we believed her. "I ate guinea pigs," she told us, "but I could never stomach monkey stew."

Once, riding muleback through the Peruvian jungle, where my grandfather worked in a mine, she saw a great tropical tree entirely covered with enormous blossoms, "a bouquet for a giant," and unbelievably beautiful butterflies, like flying orchids. Pregnant, she rode a mule for more than a week, all the way from the mine to the Andean city of Cuzco, where she awaited the birth of her first child.

"Just before the baby was born, my doctor was killed in a duel," she recalled. "But I found another one, and when your aunt Peggy was old enough, we rode back to the mine."

It was hard for us to imagine her bulk mounted on muleback, but we had no doubt that once there, she would make any mule obey. *We* certainly did. When we came to visit, she put us to work. Once we labored for several hot and itchy hours to clear a field of dry tumbleweeds, and then we piled them high and burned them in several unforgettable bonfires that shot flames up into the twilight as high as telephone poles. Afterward, we all feasted on Moon Pies and Royal Crown Cola—for she had a childlike love of cheap sweets. On less dramatic occasions, we sat around her yellow kitchen table and picked the pebbles and mudballs from several pounds of speckled pinto beans, a handful at a time. It's a good job for small fingers and sharp eyes, as my own daughters know.

"My father forbade my brothers and me to speak Spanish," Grandmama used to remark. "He couldn't understand it himself, you see."

But they spoke it anyway behind his back, she and her brothers, six wild ranch kids of a century ago. Tom, John, Bill, Jim, Joe, and Lavina. They lived hard and long, and my grandmother survived them all.

"Peggy grew up speaking Spanish, English, and Quechua," she told us. "She learned Quechua from her baby-sitter. In spite of the rumors, I never believed for a moment that those gentle people in the jungle were headhunters and cannibals. Be sure to take out the shriveled and broken beans, children, and all the ones that are unhealthy colors."

The beans were beautiful, I always thought, admiring

their color, wildly spattered rather than carefully painted, with flecks of russet, chocolate, and pink; they reminded me of beads or money or magic talismans, each one containing the source of new life. Soon they would become delicious.

"Peggy and I used to speak Spanish every night while we did the dishes, so she wouldn't forget," my grandmother went on.

A former one-room schoolteacher, she held a forceful belief in the value of education, and although the Quechua faded from my aunt's memory when the family returned to Arizona, the Spanish did not. I wish that I had been as lucky. My own Spanish is a patchwork: some learned by ear in childhood, some later in school, some during visits to Mexico as a teenager, some from my grandmother.

"Next, we'll just wash these beans," said Grandmama. "Probably we got the dirt out, but you never know. I hope we got all the rocks. They can break your teeth."

"Tell us about the time you shot yourself in the foot," we suggested.

Rattling the beans in the sink, she gave a snort of disgust. "Oh, that! That was nothing, a silly accident! I happened to pick up a pistol that your uncle Jim had filed down into a hair trigger without telling me, that's all."

Sometimes, when she was feeling indulgent, she would show us her bullet scar. But not when she wanted to get the *frijoles* boiling. She didn't, I think, really like to cook—although she had done a lot of it in her time—but she liked to eat, and there was a short list of special dishes that she cooked superlatively well.

"You can soak the beans overnight to shorten the cooking time," she said. "Or you can do them in the pressure cooker, or you can cover them with lots of water and boil 'em till they're done. I'll just add an onion and a few strips of bacon—a ham bone would be good if I had it, but I don't—and no salt till the end. Remember that. It makes *frijoles duros*."

A half dozen tight pink spearheads have split the pearly membrane of their flower sheath, and one by one the lily buds spread their six petals and trumpet their sweet scent at me. Their color shades from pale pink along the outer edges to white to green deep in their throats; the pollen settles on my desk like flour.

Even outside a house, you can smell beans cooking. The steam carries it: rich oiliness of pork, mingled with slowly dissolving onion and pungent, clayey beans make my nose tingle as I walk slowly through my grandmother's garden—all this inside my head.

My grandmother's garden was tidy, well watered, and thriving; she liked yardwork better than housework. She preferred to chop a rattlesnake's head off with a shovel rather than shoot it, for the garden tools were handier and quicker. She always did her work in a print dress of some thin fabric, one that buttoned up the front, topped off with a large conical straw hat that tied under her chin, and she never did anything slowly, but always bustled and banged her way along. Not a patient soul, she could be hot-tempered and unreasonable as well as generous and faithful.

I close my eyes and see and smell it all again: honeysuckle, rosebush, pervading moist earthiness, teeming irrigation ditches. But where did the pink lilies grow? I do remember that the gladiolus bed lay in the fertile ground beneath the big mesquite tree (its beans were inedible, but dry mesquite pods were sugar on the tongue). Late in the spring, the tall bulbs budded; early in the summer they bloomed; and every year on the last day of May my grandmother cut the flowering swords of lemon yellow, salmon pink, icy white, and tangerine. She immersed the stalks in coffee cans full of water, and drove eighty miles south to Nogales.

There she first paid a visit to the cemetery, cleaning and decorating the graves of her relatives, followed by a visit to the family ranch at Peck Canyon, where Uncle John and his son Uncle Doug ran cattle up into the mountains, where the Apaches once raided and fled, and where supposedly the Jesuit fathers buried their treasure more than two hundred years ago, when the Spanish king expelled them from their missions in New Spain. Grandmama and Uncle John sat on his porch, drinking iced tea, discussing the prices of beef and cotton, and reminiscing about their youth. Afterward she would come and visit us on her way home, her coffee cans empty, her Memorial Day duty done.

I know that the flowers on my desk came from Grandmama's garden because my aunt Peggy has told me how, a quarter of a century ago, she transplanted some of those lilies to the garden of another family ranch, which has now come down to me. And there the lilies continue to grow, thick brown stumps that support fountains of live green ribbons in spite of my neglect, for although I like flowers, I am more of a cook than a gardener. Aunt Peggy gardens; I cook beans.

I never tire of working this minor miracle, this transformation of painted beads into food. I like to watch them leave their unappetizing, pale, swollen, drowned state, where they smell like crushed grass and they fight against their fate; and then begin to relax and soften into succulent, grainy morsels swimming in a fragrant brown sauce. Bread and meat in one. New life.

"The seasoning is the important part," said my grandmother. "When they're tender, add salt to taste. Always taste! And then comes the seasoning. Some people like them full of *chile,* some add oregano and garlic and *comino* and *chorizo* and *grasa,* but this is how I do it: for about two quarts of cooked beans, one lump of brown sugar about the size of a walnut, one small spoonful of mustard, and a larger spoonful of catsup. Don't overdo it! Now let them simmer just a little while longer. Watch them. Once they're cooked and seasoned, they may stick to the bottom of the pot."

I have cooked many different kinds of beans, but I still think her *frijoles* were better than any of mine. The simplicity of the recipe—a touch of sugar to balance their natural bitterness, just a hint of fruit and spice and vinegar—smooths but does not overwhelm the true flavor of *frijoles.* They may be left whole, or mashed and refried; they may be pureed into soup; or they may be seasoned more heavily. I usually do not. Soon I will teach this recipe to my younger daughter, who likes to cook.

"When I lived at the Bosque Ranch with my brothers, the governor of Arizona once came to eat with us," my grandmother used to recall. "And when he finished, he said, 'Ma'am, I've eaten the famous beans in the Senate dining room in Washington, D.C., but yours beat them all hollow.' " A spark of mischief gleamed in her hazel eyes. "But then, we had our doubts about the governor. He sat there at my table and cleaned his fingernails with a fork! *¡Ay, Chihuahua mi tierra caramba!*"

It astonishes me sometimes to observe how closely, either deliberately or unconsciously, my aunt has modeled her life upon her mother's. Although they were both spanked for speaking Spanish in school, my aunt's bilingualism has been a treasure to her, too. In World War II it brought her a job as a Navy interpreter; later it opened many doors as she traveled; and when she was left a widow with a child to support, it provided her with a teaching specialty. For twenty years she taught children to speak, read, write, and count in both languages. Actually, they had very little choice in the matter; being my grandmother's daughter, she never doubted that her students would succeed, and most of them did. She visited their homes to do special tutoring and to insist that their mothers must stop delousing them by spraying the children's hair with Raid and putting bags over their heads. And, armed with books and pictures that she collected on her summer travels, she returned to her school, a former prisoner of war camp in the farming town of San Luis, Arizona, and she held up before her students images of the Parthenon, the Mona Lisa, and the works of the Impressionists.

My aunt bought an old house with a wire gate and a big

yard, which she transformed into a rambling garden with a floor of raked earth, and where she lived alone with her gun for decades. High in a mesquite tree, she built a fine treehouse for visiting children. She grew lilies, tulips from Holland, and rare South American plants from seeds she brought back from Peru. After she retired, she allowed herself to gain weight, and her trips became more ambitious. To see the art treasures of the Hermitage, she traveled to the Soviet Union; she cruised among the icebergs and penguins of Antarctica; she saw the Taj Mahal by moonlight.

Once we took a trip together, just the three of us, creating a small stir whenever we crossed international borders, since my grandmother was born in Arizona Territory, my aunt in Peru, and I in Mexico (where my father was working in a mine). I still don't understand why I, a chubby eight-year-old with a pixie haircut that provided a constant source of pain to my chic aunt, was swept off to Scotland with them in the summer of 1959. I don't know how any of us could afford such a trip; Grandmama must have hoped to find her Scottish roots, and insisted on involving us in her quest. We met no other Cummings; we remained tourists, Americans, and Westerners. Day after day, country by country, my cowlicks stubbornly resisted Aunt Peggy's hairspray. Yet if Grandmama meant to mark me with indelible memories, to hand something down, she succeeded, for a whiff of airplane exhaust (or hairspray) always makes me eight years old again. And many times since then, I have climbed in my mind the crumbling stone stairs of the tower of ruined Urquhart Castle on the banks of Loch Ness, near the deep caves along the lakeshore where the monster is said to lurk, and gazed in wonder at the steel gray lake and misty countryside, so utterly different from the Southwest.

The lilies on my desk continue to unfold, to wither, and to open again throughout early June, up to the day when Aunt Peggy arrives for a visit, banging on my door with her usual lack of warning. She has just returned from another trip to Scotland.

"There!" She points at the map of Inverness-shire, acquired as part of her genealogical research. She, too, has embarked on a quest. "That's where our ancestors lived, on poor little farms right beside Urquhart Castle. In 1959 we were there without knowing it!"

I look at the other place-names highlighted on the map: Tobar Ruigeard, Drumnadrochit, Pitcherle Beg. "They must have spoken Gaelic," I suggest.

Aunt Peggy isn't interested in foreign languages. I recall how in her last days my grandmother once complained to me: "People don't speak good Spanish anymore. They use all sorts of words I don't understand.

Listen!" And peeking into the hall of the hospital I discovered two old ladies chattering away in Chinese.

Suddenly my aunt bursts out: "You must think I've been very foolish."

"No, no, of course not."

"Really? Not crazy, to sell my house and spend the money for a trip on the Concorde?"

"Certainly not. Didn't you enjoy yourself?" Besides, I am sure she hasn't spent all her money on one flight.

"The pilot invited me into the cockpit," says my aunt dreamily. "I saw the curve of the earth." Abruptly she changes the subject. "I just inspected the family plot in the Nogales Cemetery, collecting names and dates, and it's a disgrace. Mother used to tend it, you know."

"Yes, I remember."

The Nogales Cemetery contains as fine a mixture of people as the town itself, or our extended family: The names on the stones are Spanish, English, French, Lebanese, Chinese, Russian, Irish, Scottish, Japanese, Korean, and Vietnamese. There are crosses and Stars of David; there are plain slabs; there are homemade cement markers. The old wooden ones have long since crumbled into dust, and some graves are unmarked. Some are unique: On the grave of a drug-smuggling pilot who died in a crash, there is a stone carved with a marijuana leaf and these words: THROUGH WHAT STRANGE SKY DO YOU FLY NOW, AMIGO?

"There's no grass, of course," says my aunt. "Just headstones and dirt. Well, grass would be impossible, I suppose. You would have to install an irrigation system. But I think I'll take up a collection among the family and get some nice clean decomposed granite to cover the graves."

"Good idea," I answer.

Wanderers who go to earth in a desert don't need grass, in my opinion, and personally I am very fond of rocks; I'll pay for my part of the granite. When my aunt rushes off on her quest, I return to my desk and think once more about gifts from the dead. My grandmother's house has burned down, and her garden, like herself, is gone to dust, yet she lives on, in words, and recipes, and flowers, and us. As I pinch off a shriveled lily to make way for the next fragrant pink bloom, I wonder if the time has come for me to become a better gardener: Maybe I should start a compost heap, buy mulch, spread fertilizer, divide my cramped bulbs, prune, rake, water. . . . Maybe I will cook another pot of beans instead; they can simmer while I write.

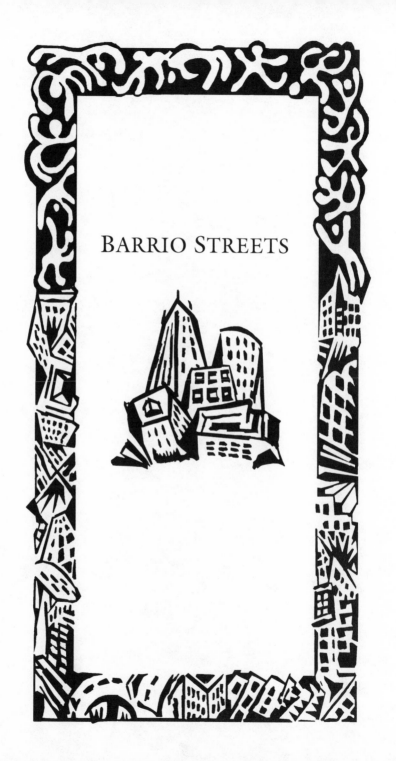

BARRIO STREETS

The increasing flow of Hispanic immigrants to the United States from the three countries of Mexico, Puerto Rico, and Cuba has enriched the nation since the mid-twentieth century. In 1951 the Mexican Farm Labor Supply Program and the Mexican Labor Agreement brought many Mexican workers to U.S. soil. In 1952 the status of Puerto Rico was changed from a U.S. territory to a commonwealth, and this allowed more and more people to move back and forth between the island and large cities on the mainland. Thousands of Cubans fled their homeland after the Cuban revolution. After immigration laws changed in 1965, Dominicans came to the United States in large numbers, too.

In the '60s, the broad sweeping demands of civil rights leaders had an effect on the political awareness of Hispanics, and one of the results of this heightened demand for justice was the developing Chicano movement. In the eastern United States, similar political upheaval occured with other Spanish-speaking groups. There was a sense of loneliness and community, individual pain and political solidarity. Life was stressful. Families were increasingly affected by low wages and clashing values, as well as the pressures of assimilation. The sense of invisibility experienced by Spanish-speaking Americans in the early decades of this century continued but began to give way to social activism and a call for organization.

A garden over concrete to recall Caribbean places . . . a beautiful bolero . . . learning English to move ahead . . . a poem about a favorite aunt . . . In this part of *Barrio Streets Carnival Dreams,* contemporary artists share with us new gifts—of advice, of poetry and love, of social justice and hope—inspired by the old. Our lives today are shaped by many of these gifts, contributions that are being noticed more and more throughout America.

❊ ❊ ❊

VERANO

FELIPE GALINDO-FEGGO

⠃⠃ ⠃⠃ ⠃⠃

THE SENSES OF SUMMER:
HEAR THE BEAT

OSCAR HIJUELOS

*Oscar Hijuelos was born to Cuban parents in New York
City. He is the first American of Hispanic heritage to win
the Pulitzer Prize in fiction for his novel,* The Mambo
Kings Play Songs of Love. *His most recent novel is*
Mr. Ives' Christmas.

Around mid-June, when it starts feeling like summer in
New York and it's a Friday night, windows open and I
hear a thousand musicians jamming. From a twelfth-floor
apartment on 106th Street—Duke Ellington Boulevard—
I can hear just about every merengue and salsa party for
miles; in the distance, yellow-lit tenement windows and
the silhouettes of twirling, hugging dancers, happy in
courtship; I can hear the mambos of Tito Puente, the bo-
leros of Beny Moré, the new-age Latin of Gloria Estefan
and Ruben Blades.

Man, it's hot, but now and then someone pulls out a
trumpet or a bongo drum and improvises over the music;
there's always a happy squeal of laughter, hand-clapping,

whistling, a claves beat out on a Coke bottle, and these sounds rise up out of that particular window, joining the sounds of another party; and they join up with the music of yet another party and this multiplies into infinity so that the atmosphere gets crazy with mambo, merengue, chachachá—a spontaneous and new multirhythmed, multikeyed music, with crooners and *soneros* belting out their songs, until it sounds like everybody in the world is a singer.

I imagine a hundred orchestras floating on a cloud over the rooftops, and now and then this is cut by a police or fire truck siren, or by the impressive roar of sanitation trucks working for the city good. This is joined by some rap or hip-hop music from the tape decks of young entrepreneurs cruising the streets in their $20,000 Jeeps. Just then, one of my neighbors turns on his million-dollar stereo, and now I'm hearing Coltrane on top of everything else, and that's very cool, I guess. But when I walk into another room to watch TV, some kid in my building opens up with his brand-new Fender electric guitar and amplifier, and now there's no quiet place to go, and it's suddenly July, when the kids on the street are shooting off firecrackers.

I begin to feel a little nutty and crave earplugs, the way I did one afternoon five years ago when my girlfriend and

I, out at the Rockaway Beach for a little soothing ocean air and the soft murmur of waves, found ourselves surrounded by an army of raging boom boxes, each as big as a closet and louder than the explosion of an atomic bomb.

So, going on the theory that sound rises and that it will be quieter on the street, I take a walk. Down by the corner *bodega* a group of men are sitting out on the sidewalk playing cards and watching a boxing match or baseball game; kids are playing tag or stickball. On the corner is a bar with the click-clack of pool cues and rock 'n' roll, the roar of Sports Channel and Budweiser and Coke ads. Then the sing-song chimes and a Mister Softee truck bring little kids running in circles and shouting, "Mommee, Mommee!"

Walking along Broadway, I pass the jazz bars and the wail of the saxes follows me for blocks. Around 110th Street, some blues band has set up in front of a church, down another block a country group is singing Hank Williams tunes, and some preacher's shouting through a mike about the resurrection of the flesh, while a few yards away, some poor bewildered and ragged fellow is muttering loudly to himself about a conspiracy to steal his soul; I stop by a bookstore to check out the latest, and there I am soothed by Bach, which takes me back to a thousand Sunday masses at my old Catholic church.

Having killed some time, I'm on Duke Ellington Boulevard again, and for a moment I flash on the great Duke himself. I can imagine him on a summer weekend in 1937, all decked out in a soft silk suit and, behind the wheel of a pearly white Oldsmobile, ready to take a quiet drive in the country. That's what I want, I think while riding the elevator home.

With the next day's newspapers spread out on a table before me, I sit daydreaming again; Duke Ellington, whose music I have always loved, gives me a ring on the telephone and says, "It'll be a little warm tomorrow, what say you come along with me, to my place upstate?"

A moment of calm, even while the orchestras outside my window are still having their battle of the bands. A moment of respite while love is thriving, feet are moving, and cops are sirening, and I think about my friends who live in quieter places: an ex-girlfriend with whom I had spent several summers, going to county fairs and tending to her garden; another friend with a house out on Long Island and the beach not too far away, where I could splash in the surf; and another friend, way upstate with the twitter of birdsong.

Wouldn't it be nice to get away?

As if on cue, the next morning, I hear from my older brother, who invites me out to his place on Staten Island, on a quiet street, across from a cemetery, where he has a little yard and shady trees.

I head downtown on the noisy, clamorous subway with its crazy musicians and screeching speakers, and then hit the ferryboat for a pleasant ride to Staten Island. And soon enough I'm sitting out in my brother's backyard. The only sounds I hear are those of an occasional passing car, a lawnmower mowing away for the good of lawns, and the sprinkler watering some quiet, well-behaved plants.

The truth? It's great to get away, but after a few hours of peace I always begin to get a craving for the sounds of home.

HIJO DE LA MALINCHE

RAÚL NIÑO

Raúl Niño is a poet of Mexican heritage who now lives in Chicago, Illinois. When he was ten years old he crossed the Mexican border with his mother to live in Texas. He is the author of, among other books, Breathing Light.

La Malinche was Malintzin, a woman born of a native Mexican royal family. Her mother sold her into slavery, and she was later given to the Spanish conquistador Hernando Cortéz. They had a son, and she was married off to one of Cortéz's soldiers. She is a symbol of racial and cultural mixing in Mexico, as well of property that is given away, sold off.

¡América!
Yo soy americano
tengame en tu corazón
the same as I have you
in my mestizo soul.
We are all immigrants

fallen from the same sky
into a land claimed
long before Columbus.

I am not the stoic statue
advertised on vacation posters.
I am flesh,
como un hijo de la Malinche.
I pray to our old gods
conveniently renamed
for my salvation.

La historia de mi raza
is older than this colonized nation.
My blood runs in rivers
no border can divide,
in me oppressor and oppressed
drink from the same cup.

My bones a frame
that my ancestors built
with pain and calloused dreams,
they passed on to me
the language of the sun in
an immigrant's voice.

Nunca nos desaparecimos
de nuestra tierra,
sino nuestra tierra
se desapareció de nosotros.

Somos americanos,
all of us!
We live in a country of sacrifice
that tries to yank
our hearts from the body
of this land.
¡América!
Don't turn your head away
don't close your eyes.
¡América!
If I am illegal,
Then we are all illegal!

FLORENCIA

DAVID HERNANDEZ

David Hernandez is a poet, educator, narrator, and founder of "Street Sounds"—a performing arts group that infuses poetry and music with folk, jazz, and Afro-Latin elements. He lives in Chicago.

I will try to tell it
without remorse or
impassioned language
so you can hear it
deep in your heart forever.
  My aunt Florencia Marquéz
  was 20 when she began working
  for an American company in Puerto Rico.
  The company was taking advantage of a
  cheap-wage, tax-free economic program
  called Operation Bootstrap created in the '50s
  to get Puerto Ricans back in the workforce
  after having their agricultural jobs
  eliminated by industry.

My aunt Florencia Marquéz
had river green eyes and
mountain brown skin.
Sometimes the women who worked
for the company would take maternity leaves
and the officials did not like this.
So Operation Bootstrap implemented an
island-wide sterilization program since
it was cheaper than day care centers.
The women would go to the hospital,
give birth, and have their fallopian tubes tied
in the process without their consent.
This was done to my aunt
after my cousin Anita was born,
and after grieving for a while,
my aunt went back to work.
She eventually saved money,
moved to Chicago, and got a better job.
My cousin Anita and I grew up together
on the city's North Side.
Around 1962 when Anita was sixteen,
she got pregnant and died from a coat-hanger
operation because abortions were illegal
at that time.
She had river-green eyes
and mountain brown skin.

After grieving for a while
my aunt returned to Puerto Rico
where Anita was buried and went
back to work for the same company
that sterilized her years before.

      My aunt Florencia Marquéz is an old woman now
      who enjoys the island breezes from her
      rocking chair on the veranda.
But if you place your ear
close to her chest,
you can hear the ocean like a
hollow seashell on the sand.

      I have nothing more to say.

YOUNG DEVILS GARDEN WALL MURAL
ALBERT RIVERA

I learned about the Young Devils oasis from reading a description of the single-lot garden that buses, cars, and pedestrians pass every day on Madison Avenue in New York City. The description was taken from a longer essay written by Mary Frances Hickey, and published in New York *magazine. She explains that the Young Devils was the name given to a stickball league and that one of the members of the league, Pedro Velez, persuaded "Albert Rivera, a shy young man with no formal art training, to design and paint the spectacular murals which delight viewers in cars and on the Madison Avenue bus." Here is a detail of the navy blue sea he painted as a backdrop for the flowers and the vegetables that "the girls of past and present generations now harvest."*

The majestic bright red rose in the center of this photo is, I believe, a Hermosa, the "beautiful" name of a particular rose variety that grows exceptionally well near the waltzing, waltzing Caribbean Sea. The dark color behind the fence slats is actually a deep, rich blue. The best way, of course, to see murals like this is up close.

■ ■ ■

LEAVING YBOR CITY

JAIME MANRIQUE

Jaime Manrique, of Colombian heritage, is the author of two novels, Colombian Gold *and* Latin Moon in Manhattan, *as well as poetry, plays, and essays.*

The summer I finished high school
Mother and I worked in the same factory
in Ybor City, the black section of town.

Mami sewed all day
in silence, she knew
only a few words in English.
I worked alone, sorting out huge containers
of soiled hospital linen
and I despised every moment of it.
I was eighteen; Mami nearly fifty.

After work, we took the bus home.
As the suffocating heat
lifted, and the mango tree
in our yard released fruity
scents and yielded shadow

the languorous stretch
before dark
was a time to forget the factory
to become human.

The apartment we lived in on Elmore Street
had linoleum floors
and termites in the furniture.
After our TV dinner
—we were so new in America these
dinners seemed another miracle of technology—
mother visited her friend Hortencia,
a Cuban refugee so overweight
she could not walk to our house
after a day of piecework.
We had no television, no telephone,
so I sat on the terrace
watched the elevated highway
next to the house and read
novels that transported me
far away from Ybor City.

On Saturday afternoons, I walked
to the old library in downtown Tampa
where I discovered, in Spanish,
Manuel Puig's *Betrayed by Rita Hayworth.*

I read this book at night
and during breaks at the factory:
a novel with a homosexual boy hero
that made me dream of glamorous
MGM Technicolor musicals and goddesses
in slinky glittering gowns.
I was young.

Sitting on the porch
as dusk deepened
punctured by fireflies
darting stars weaving
in and out of the mangoes
I dreamt of distant cities
of going to college, of writing
books, of leading a life
that had nothing to do with a factory,
not knowing
I would journey
away from Ybor City
exiled from the world of my mother
yet still be a survivor.

It's only now, when I think back
on the youth I was
that I can feel

heartache for my innocence
for my mother's silent fortitude
for our unspoken fears;
for lives that were hard
but rich in dreams.

A REMEMBRANCE OF *ITACATE*

PATRICIA QUINTANA

In her beautiful cookbook, Feasts of Life, *Mexican chef Patricia Quintana shares traditions, memories, family history, and recipes with her readers. One of the most memorable characters in her story is Mamanena, the name by which Ms. Quintana refers to her grandmother. Apparently, the two had an especially trusting friendship. It was Mamanena who taught Patricia the tradition of* itacate, *described by Patricia herself.*

I remember how Mamanena taught me about the *itacate,* the bundle of succulent foods to be carried away and eaten in another place. Many times, secretly, she put aside for me a few little Monterey tamales (my weakness) and a slice of cake with meringue. If others asked for seconds, she would present me with the *itacate,* all wrapped in its little bundle, whispering in my ear that there was nothing as delicious as a warmed-over tidbit. Of course, this generosity was not reserved just for me. She often prepared bundles with ample portions for those who came to her house, not only to parties but even to her simplest meals, thus continuing the tradition of the *itacate,* a gesture of trust, affection, and goodwill. To this day, when Mamanena tells me incidents of her life unfamiliar to me, I am suddenly ten years old again, and everything this wonderful woman does and says seems to be out of a storybook. The grandmother who taught me to love the world and its beauty and who initiated me into this universe of surprises and magic called gastronomy also brought me to the calling that makes me sure I am alive.

BOLEROBOMBABUGALÚCONGACHARANGACORRIDO

A GLOSSARY OF SOME COMMON TERMS IN LATIN MUSIC

JOHN STORM ROBERTS

During the 1940s and '50s, Latin American music had tremendous influence on the United States. In the 1940s Machito's Afro-Cubans set a standard of both quality and popularity. They also had large followings. Music, always an important part of Latin American culture, was now being enjoyed by its American practitioners and translators. And while many musical styles were brought to North America by Spanish-speaking immigrants, it was Cuban music that had the greatest influence on the rest of the country.

BOLERO

The Cuban bolero, originally a midpaced form for string trios, became very popular internationally, usually in a slower and more sentimental form. The modern bolero is a lush, romantic, popular song form, largely distinct from salsa, and very few singers are equally good at both.

BOMBA

Originally a Puerto Rican three-drum dance form of marked west-central African ancestry, the bomba is especially associated with the Puerto Rican village of Loíza Aldea. It is still played there in its old form at the festival of Santiago, and New York Puerto Rican folk revival companies also perform it from time to time. Even in the dance band form introduced by Rafael Cortijo in the late 1950s, the bomba's melodies, as well as its rhythmic pulse, are strongly African.

BUGALÚ, LATIN

The Latin bugalú was a somewhat simplified and more sharply accented mambo with English lyrics, singing that combined Cuban and black inflections, and R&B–influenced solos. For a few years the bugalú and the lesser-known Puerto Rican rhythm jala jala, were staples of the Latin Soul movement.

CHACHACHÁ

The chachachá is said by some to have derived from the second section of the danzón, by others to be a slower mambo. It was sometimes called a "double mambo" in New York because its basic dance step was the mambo with a double step between the fourth to first beats. The chachachá developed around 1953 in the hands of Cuban charangas, most notably the Orquesta Aragón.

CHARANGA

Cuban dance orchestras consisting of flute backed by fiddles, piano, bass, and timbales, charangas tended to play different dances from the Afro-Cuban *conjuntos,* the most characteristic being the danzón. Charangas ranged from the large society units to small street bands. Modern charangas use bongo and conga in the rhythm section and have taken on many more Afro-Cuban elements than their predecessors.

CONGA RHYTHM

The Cuban conga was originally a Carnival dance march from Santiago de Cuba with a heavy fourth beat, but the rhythm is common to Carnival music in many parts of the new world. The conga rhythm is more easily simplified than most Cuban rhythms and was a natural for nightclub floorshows. It never became permanent in mainstream Latin music, though Eddie Palmieri introduced a modified version called the mozambique in the late 1960s.

CORRIDO

This Mexican and Chicano ballad form developed during the nineteenth century and reached its peak during the first half of the twentieth century. Pure folk ballads in their simplicity, detail, and deadpan performing style, the corridos were the history books, news reports, and editorials of the illiterate. They chronicled the whole of the Mexican civil war; almost all notable crimes, strikes, and other political events; and a hundred other subjects besides.

HABANERA

Cuban dance of Spanish origin and the first major Latin influence on U.S. music around the time of the Spanish-American War, the habanera provided the rhythmic basis of the modern tango, which makes its influence in twentieth-century American music difficult to trace.

LATIN JAZZ

This form is a hybrid of jazz and Latin music. The term could cover anything from a Cuban number with a couple of Louis Armstrong phrases to a straight jazz number with a conga, but is best confined to crosses with a more or less full Latin rhythm section, or one combining several Latin and jazz elements and an instrumental frontline.

MAMBO

This Afro-Cuban form came out of the Congolese religious cults. The big band mambo of the 1940s and 1950s developed characteristic contrasting brass and sax riffs, which many musicians regard as stemming from the last section of the guaracha (a Cuban song form that became a popular salsa style).

MARIACHI

Mexican strolling groups of (usually) semiprofessional musicians, mariachis originally were string orchestras. Since the 1940s they have become trumpet-led ensembles. Their name stems from a corruption of the French *mariage,* since they were frequently hired for weddings.

MERENGUE

Though dances by this name are found in many countries, the merengue is originally from the Dominican Republic, where it dates back at least to the early nineteenth century. The modern merengue has a notably brisk and snappy 2/4 rhythm, with a flavor very different from the somewhat more flowing Cuban and jaunty Puerto Rican dances. The country form, for accordion, tambora drum, metal scraper, and voice, is heard everywhere in the Dominican Republic. The big band version, of Dominican bands like Johnny Ventura's and Felix del Rosario's, is often heard at New York concerts.

PLENA

An Afro–Puerto Rican urban island song said to have been developed in the south-central city of Ponce during World War I. The plena has four- or six-line verses with a refrain. Lyrical content is social comment, satire, or humor. Instrumentation has ranged from percussion through accordian or guitar-led groups to various dance band formats. Its most famous composer and exponent was Manual Jiménez, known as Canario. It has been a minor influence on salsa through the work of Rafael Cortijo in the late 1950s and Willie Colón in the 1970s.

RANCHERA

The ranchera, developed in the nationalist theater of the post-1910 revolution period in Mexico, became very much the equivalent of U.S. commercial country music. Professional singers developed an extremely emotional style, one of whose characteristics is a held note at the end of a line, culminating in a "dying fall" that could drop a third or more. Rancheras became an important part of Chicano music from the 1950s onward as it moved from a folk-popular form to a greater professionalism.

RUMBA

Most of what Americans call rumbas were forms of the son, which swept Cuba in the 1920s. The Cuban rumba was a secular drum form with many variants, including the güagüancó and the columbia, though modern musicians tend to regard all these as separate. Its descendent variations can be heard in New York parks any summer weekend, played by groups called rumbas or rumbones. By analogy, a percussion passage in a salsa number, or a percussion-only jam session, is sometimes called a rumba or rumbon.

SON

The son is perhaps the oldest, and certainly the classic, Afro-Cuban form, an almost perfect balance of African and Hispanic elements. Originating in Oriente province, it surfaced in Havana around World War I and became a popular urban music played by string-and-percussion quartets and septets. Almost all the numbers Americans called rumbas were, in fact, sones. The rhythm of the son is strongly syncopated, with a basic chicka-CHUNG pulse.

TANGO

Probably the world's best-known dance after the waltz, the modern tango developed in Argentina at the beginning of the twentieth century. It took its rhythm from the Cuban habanera and the Argentinian milonga, and its name probably from the Spanish *tango andaluz*.

DANCING FOR JOY

LYDA APONTE de ZACKLIN

I have known Lyda Aponte de Zacklin for twelve years, nearly as long as I have lived in New York City. She is someone for whom I reserve that very special name of friend. Perhaps most stunning about her is the strength of her character, the depth of her wisdom. But I will never forget a time when she surprised me at a small festive gathering at her home. I was one of several invited guests, and I was the only gringa *in the group, surrounded by Venezuelan friends who were singing and playing the guitar. It happened that each of us had to improvise a song on the spot and sing to the others. Once I'd gotten over my initial shyness, I enjoyed the intense sense of community and sharing. And when it was Lyda's turn, well, she danced so beautifully that we all just stared. Lyda Aponte de Zacklin, a scholar, essayist, and dancer, is a diplomat at the Venezuelan Mission at the United Nations.*

I was born in a culture for which singing and dancing seemed the most natural way of showing our inner feelings. Passions, loves, joy, and grief could find their most profound expression in a dance, in a song.

I have always cherished this aspect of my heritage as a spiritual gift that allows me to be at peace with myself—to feel the joy and reassurance of belonging to a particular place in a vast world. Sometimes I think or even feel that the most intimate rhythm of my heart is somehow related to the music of immemorial dances and songs. But in a more tangible way I can also feel the presence of time or even of dreams that were forever caught in the echoes of my mother's voice in the nursery songs that I later sang for my children.

> Arroró mi vida
> arroró mi amor
> que se duerme el niño
> de mi corazón

Nevertheless, I wasn't aware that my children, who were educated in international surroundings, could see a distinctive sign of my own culture in the songs and dances I sometimes used to express my feelings.

My then-six-year-old son had invited a group of his classmates to our home. I sat near them while they were involved in a quiet game, and I continued writing my history paper. I contemplated a paragraph that I had written and was so pleased with it that I stood up and started dancing. I will never forget that moment. A few seconds had passed before I was interrupted by the most perplexed audience. The children looked up at me with eyes full of amazement and disbelief. I felt myself blushing like a little girl, incapable of saying a single word, when I heard the most reassuring and simple statement made by my son: "She does that, because she's Venezuelan."

CARNIVAL DREAMS

On the brink of the twenty-first century, people from almost all the Latin American nations have found a home in North America. In the late 1970s and 1980s, the disturbing violence in some Central American and South American nations sent many people north. People escaping political repression in their homelands came to the United States—Guatemalans, Salvadorans, Nicaraguans, Argentinians, Chileans. And there were other nationals who chose to make North America their home, such as Mexicans, Puerto Ricans, and Cubans. Peruvians, Venezuelans, Uruguayans, Bolivians, and Ecuadoreans. In the last decades of the twentieth century, increasing numbers of Spanish-speaking Americans are assuming leading roles in the arts, education, and professions that were previously off limits. All are creating a vivid pattern of art and culture throughout the country, thought of as "Latino." And Latino customs and foods are being embraced by Americans of all classes and backgrounds. Salsa has become more popular than ketchup and tacos are as pleasing to everyone's tastebuds as grilled hamburgers. While many troubles beset Latinos in their daily lives in this land, there is also a bright awareness and pride in Latino culture. What will Latinos take with them from their *antepasados* and cultural icons today into the next millennium?

Hope defined in lyrics for a guitar tune . . . photography to shatter bleakness in a basement studio . . . Latino style in a classy dress . . . taquerías in L.A. The last part of this collection explores the contributions that a new generation will make to the future of the United States, once again passing valuable gifts that we can only dream about to Americans of coming generations.

■ ■ ■

SELF-DEFINITION

ROSIE PEREZ

Rosie Perez has appeared in many films, among them, Do the Right Thing, White Men Can't Jump, *and* It Could Happen to You.

"I'm Hispanic. I'm not Spanish. Spanish is when you're from Spain. I'm not European. I'm not Castilian. I am of Latin descent. I am from the Caribbean island of Puerto Rico. I am Puerto Rican from New York, I'm Latina. Hispanic is the Spanish-speaking and Latin American living in the U.S. That is me. It wasn't a conscious decision that I made. When people ask me 'What are you, are you mixed, are you half black, half white, are you Spanish and something else?' I go no, I'm Puerto Rican. . . .

"Growing up in Brooklyn I got a real sense of self. When you live in Brooklyn, there's so many strong ethnic communities that you have a sense of belonging, you have roots, and you feel very comfortable in those roots, and you feel very comfortable because everyone else is like you too. . . . And, it's okay."

✠ ✠ ✠

SELF-PORTRAIT

RAQUEL JARAMILLO

*Raquel Jaramillo, whose parents are Colombian, is a
graphic designer and illustrator. She grew up and
currently lives in New York City.*

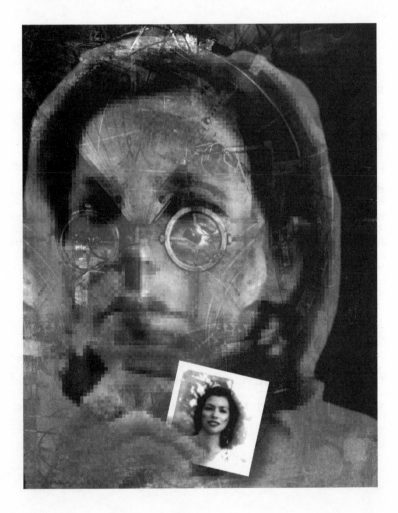

FROM THE SOUTH BRONX TO GROTON

JOHANNA VEGA

Johanna Vega is the daughter of immigrants from Puerto Rico and Spain. She is a poet and essayist. In the following essay she explores the difficulty of being a "minority" student in the hallowed ambience of an Eastern prep school.

I think it was in the dining hall when I finally realized that my parents were going to leave me, that they weren't staying there with me. The school provided a lunch for parents before they were asked to say good-bye to the sons and daughters they were leaving behind. At the lunch table in the Groton School Dining Hall, we were sitting with a family from California, and it occurred to me that I and my parents looked glaringly different. In fact, we were sitting with serious Groton legacy material from the 1950s, and the girl next to me was the daughter of an alumnus who, as I found out later, was a schoolmate and good friend of the headmaster's. They had been on the same ice hockey team at Groton. Yes, this man and the headmaster went back, way back. He was rich, upper class, from California, and my father was sitting next to him. I remember looking at them both and wondering how farfetched a conversation would be between this businessman/Groton graduate and my father, the long-shoreman from Puerto Rico. Thinking back on it now, I understand why my father rushed through his meal as he did. But I can't even begin to fathom what it was like for my mother, who barely understands English, much less speaks it. Looking around the table, I realized that not only were my parents going to leave me there, but I had nothing in common with this place and didn't really know what the hell I was doing there. My parents wouldn't have to deal with the differences because they were splitting. But I was stuck.

Later in the day, after my parents had left, we got in line for supper to get barbecued hamburgers. It was a picnic supper, probably intended to make us feel comfortable and informal. But filed in line, with preppies in front of me, behind me, and next to me, I began to feel different again. I was still wearing those Carter's undershirts that my mother ceremoniously bought for me, hoping to postpone my puberty, and the little sleeves kept popping out of my tank top so I kept pushing them back in, thinking that all these girls were probably wearing training bras. There I was, wearing the latest Bronx fashion: a

Day-Glo orange tank top with my name inscribed in electric blue letters. I felt and looked like a kid, underdeveloped in every sense. All these big North American girls were taller and really developed, and maybe even socially experienced, and here I was, still my mom's little *"rabito,"* her little tail, as she often put it—just a sheltered little thing finding out that life wasn't like home all the time, at least not anymore it wasn't.

From the moment I was born until I was eleven, I grew up in the South Bronx, in the very worst area that you can find in the South Bronx; outsiders call it Fort Apache. Then we moved to New Jersey, to the suburbs, because we weren't eligible to live in the projects anymore. My father was making more money, so we were asked to leave because we didn't need that kind of help. We went to Elizabeth, a small city next to Newark. It didn't work out there because my mother found it hard to adjust, so we moved back to the inner city and lived in the Bronx again, on the Grand Concourse. My father was mugged several times at gunpoint, his car was stolen, our apartment was broken into, and meanwhile my mother clutched at me more and more, protecting her little cub from all the dangers that lurked in the Bronx.

While I was in junior high school, we moved again,

this time to Parkchester in the north of the Bronx. It was an improvement. Because it was a residential community, it was a big change, but we still had our friends, the minorities around us, plus the novelty of now living among Jews, too. However, I still went to school in the South Bronx, where the crime seemed to worsen by the day. I remember my best friend was mugged. They ripped off a clarinet he had borrowed from school. I remember how he came into class in tears, shaking as he told our home-room teacher what had happened. The only reason I was spared this crime was my mother's constant and doting presence. I never rode the subway by myself until I got back from Groton when I was eighteen. That was how much she protected me.

Despite this environment, I was a fun-loving, perky kid in junior high and before. I was in an accelerated program designed to skip students from seventh to ninth grade. I was constantly involved in school plays, and I always had a number of friends to hang out with. I even had a clique. I hung out with kids who were in the Special Progress program—the highest-ranking class. We were the brat pack—the smarty-pants—and heck, did we know it. We were always on top, setting the highest reading and math scores for the entire district. It gave us a feeling of power in relation to the other students. I certainly developed enough of an ego in junior high to feel really confident about myself, even cocky in a way.

When I was invited to Groton to visit, I felt really great and special. My affair with Groton had actually started earlier, back in seventh grade. A Better Chance (ABC) had talked to several minority students about the virtues of prep schools, so we accepted an invitation to visit a few boarding schools. We spent a night at Groton, and I thought it was great because everything was beautiful. It was like being invited to go to camp for four years. After that visit, I had dreams about walking in the woods instead of walking on asphalt in the inner city. Groton seemed like Wonderland, and I guess I thought I could be a giant Alice.

For me it was either the Bronx High School of Science or Groton, and I already knew I wanted Groton. I had a notion that if I went to Groton the experience would somehow change me and make me a better person than if I stayed at home and lived with my family. By that time I did have a vague understanding of the upper-class white world as distinct from the lower-income Hispanic world in which I was brought up. I watched television. Television brought the elite white world into our Bronx living room, and there I learned how different my family was from the Carringtons, the Ewings, and the oil-magnate-family soap operas so popular in the early eighties. As lame as it sounds, you see *Dallas* and *Dynasty* and you are influenced by the glitz and glamour. Groton looked like one of those country clubs. If I could go to Groton, I could not only get a ticket into college, I could get a ticket into that world.

Things were really bad with my first roommate right from the start because she and I weren't getting along. She had complained to the housemistress that my father kept looking at her when he helped me move into the room. She never articulated her fears directly to me. But she would ignore me in the room, and it was hard to talk to her. Her friends would come into the room; I would try to start a conversation, and they would acknowledge for a moment and then start laughing among themselves and eventually exclude me from their inside jokes. Tensions grew between us. At the time, and actually for four years, I was severely homesick. My first roommate must have thought I was a crybaby for wanting to be home with my parents, calling them every night and crying over the phone. She often told her friends that she was happy to be away from home, finally.

During the first two months in the dorms the differences between the other girls and me were engulfing my life. Underhanded references to "that Puerto Rican girl living upstairs" became a torment for me, and I cringed whenever I heard them. There were strange looks exchanged whenever I entered my room and my roommate and her friends happened to be there. I knew something was going on; to them I was a poor Hispanic and thus foreign, unapproachable, maybe even untouchable. At a dorm meeting, I exposed these feelings, telling everyone that while I might look different, I wouldn't bite their heads off. I explained to them that it was just harder for me to be at Groton because I couldn't relate to so many things, and that they needed to know that when they approached me. In the end, however, my roommate and I had to separate, and the whole dorm ended up switching roommates as well. All this may have been typical adolescent behavior, but even so it certainly made life hard for me. My housemistress dismissed it as "going through a cruel stage." My job was to grin and bear it, and wait for them to reach a more mature level, a level at which I would become more human and less "minority" in their eyes.

My best friend at Groton turned out to be the girl who became my roommate as a result of that switch. There was a lot of tension at that time because her father had lung cancer. One day she and I got into a fistfight about whether our room door should be left open or closed during study hall. Afterward, I began to admire and appreciate her, and she became my best friend. We finally let things out into the open instead of bottling them up. In a strange way that was a real relief. One of the things I appreciated about her was that she had the gall to punch me physically and not keep wounding me emotionally. At Groton there was a lot of psychic wounding and not enough relating to me as a person of flesh and blood.

As unhappy as I was at Groton, my parents were adamant about my staying there. The high schools in the Bronx are not as good, and my parents thought that I'd be tainted by the experience there. They preferred the idea of their daughter going to a very nice, clean, classy school where they wouldn't have to worry about me being introduced to drugs, sex, and all those things. My staying at Groton became more and more convenient for my parents; it was hellish for me.

The bus rides from Groton to New York always had the strange effect of empowerment for me. I remember the bus carried us into the South Bronx before dropping us off on 86th Street and 5th Avenue on the Upper East Side, where many of the students lived. The journey had its own metamorphosis for me. The contrast between the South Bronx and Upper East Side of Manhattan was as awkward as my relationship with Groton. I remember feeling a pride when the bus passed through my old neighborhood. A rush of nostalgia wrenched my heart, reminding me that it was merely a past I was now sharing with Groton on this bus. Someday, I would become as much an outsider to the Bronx as they were now. Yes, time would tell. Nonetheless, back then I couldn't grasp this, and I would tell the kids sitting around me, "See that school, the one with graffiti, where the bum is pissing—I went to school there." Those young, healthy faces looked outside the bus windows and then looked at me with astonishment and, yes, maybe a little admiration. Did I feel like the voyager, the traveled one, the insider and yet, all at once, the outsider? I suspect the Bronx they saw in passing on the bus resembled a dark forest to which only I could be admitted and welcomed. I felt powerful as I often whispered to myself. "Let's see you all try to cross the street in this neighborhood with your shiny penny loafers and Harris tweed sports jackets. Yes, let's see you find out how really powerless you are in these mean streets."

After I had been at Groton a while, I noticed that all the big girls were hanging out together. There was a separation between us that got wider and wider as time went on. You were in real trouble if you were wimpy looking, poor, Hispanic, or glaringly different. I was all those things, or felt that I was. This realization was painful because most girls there had things that I didn't have. We even dressed differently. They wore Laura Ashley dresses and I wore Lee dungarees. I had a very limited wardrobe, while these girls seemed to have it all. I still remember the trillions of wool sweaters stacked neatly, one on top of the other, in the shelves on the walls. My shelves were always bare except for one or two acrylic sweaters that I wore alternately. Their clothes and their mannerisms made them appear more powerful in my eyes and, in the process, made me feel inferior and unworthy of attending Groton. This place was made for them, not for me.

As a result, I was stripped of my own sexuality, or perhaps I stripped myself. At Groton I didn't consider myself a woman or a man, I was a Puerto Rican—a South Bronx Puerto Rican. I couldn't conceive of any other identity. I earned my name at Groton as that; people knew what I stood for. I wasn't really treated as a girl there. There was no chance of dating, not even with the other Hispanic kid there. We were just not attracted to each other. So we were the last Hispanic boy and girl stranded on this island called Groton. Do you have to be attracted to each other just because you're from the same place? I had crushes on boys at Groton, like every young girl does, but I always knocked down those fantasies with the knowledge that it could never happen; it was taboo even to think about it for too long.

When I was at Groton, I believed that many of the kids there had been sent to tennis camps. I fantasized that there they had undergone a sort of upper-class boot camp to prepare them for prep school. I was a complete novice at this kind of life, so I kept falling behind. I was becoming lazier. For a time I didn't have enough incentive to keep going. After a while, my experience told me that being Puerto Rican somehow meant they expected less from me and led me to question why I should work harder if they didn't expect to get any results anyway. At every juncture any hope that I had seemed to be chopped down. I was behind academically and athletically. I had nothing to offer Groton. And what could Groton offer someone with no hope of catching up?

I remember the first English paper that was returned to me; the grade was a C−. I cried and cried and then went to my headmistress. I asked if I were really that bad a writer? She told me that while I had been tops in my other schools, I was now bottom. Groton was a different, tougher place, and I had a lot of catching up to do. That advice was repeated to me over and over again every year. There was no specific way to catch up, and yet the teachers kept saying that. I didn't know where to begin or where it was supposed to end. It was all very abstract. "You have catching up to do"—but in what way?

I kept my mouth shut in classes for a long time because I was embarrassed to speak up. The boys in particular were intimidating. They had a command of the language, having gone to private schools all their lives. There was no way that I could catch up to them, that I could learn their rhetoric. I didn't want to make a fool of myself in the classes so I kept quiet. I began to fall behind in all my schoolwork and could not keep up the same pace that these kids could. I was a slower learner than they were. There seemed to be so many things to do that I had never done at home. Even sit-down dinners and chapel in the morning were new and demanding.

There was one specific attempt to help, an effort that went well for a month or two though I don't remember learning anything from it because I felt so hostile toward the fact that I needed help. I was also not comfortable with the person giving me the help. My housemistress was trying to work with me, and I already had too much contact with her. The tutoring started just after the fist-fight with my roommate, and all I wanted to do was get that woman out of my hair as soon as possible. Instead I saw her every minute of the goddamn day. As a result, the tutoring fell apart.

Looking back on Groton, I realize now that the teachers at Groton struggled with my whole attitude. Many of them couldn't communicate with me. That was not true of a counselor at the school. There was a different relationship between the two of us. I started seeing her when I was a ninth grader, and she became the sole support system I had at Groton. Once a week we had a forty-minute session and I would tell her how I felt, how depressed I was, how much I hated it there, and how I wanted to leave. That went on for four years. She was wonderful. She was my savior at Groton. She gave me a lot of nurturing and love.

I suppose that every student has to find a way to survive at school, and I had to find something other than the counselor to get through Groton. Art and religion became my food there; my bread and water. A little picture of Jesus Christ that I had acquired on a pilgrimage to a religious site in the Bronx called "La Gruta" became my lucky charm, my connection to home, my psychic connection to mother and father. I saved this picture of Jesus in a little clear box, and I tucked it under my pillow every night after I said my prayers. Jesus Christ and the Virgin Mary became my saviors, my dependable icons, my imaginary friends. My mother had also given me some religious medals when I was ten. I wore them all the time, even when I was jogging. I still have memories of running through the woods, hearing these medals clink together, fearful that I would never see my mother again. Even now, I can't stand this sound.

In my first year at Groton, I managed to get a part as a maid in Anton Chekov's play *The Bear*. I thought it was the most gripping thing that I had ever done, the way the audience laughed and cheered me on at the end. It was the most fun I had ever had at Groton, and I felt really proud of myself for a long time afterward. But that was the first and last time I would appear on stage in a school production. I wanted to pursue acting, but as the years went by all the parts were taken by a certain breed of student—long and smallboned and very elegant-looking female students. Of course, I never fit into that category. I realized what was going on when an Indian girl from New Delhi also never got to act, because she was dark and didn't fit the parts. Students who looked different were lucky if they got to play the maids. This loss was very significant to me because I loved acting; one other thing that mattered to me was chopped off.

I did discover art, and sculpture in particular, at Groton. My involvement began during my freshman year with a project that we did involving food in a freshman studio art class. I made a small artichoke out of clay, since my mother comes from the south of Spain and made a lot of dishes with artichokes. My father is from Puerto Rico, so we also ate rice, beans, plantains, and other tropical specialties. My final piece was a clay sculpture of rice, beans, artichokes, and a pork chop—foods typical of my hybrid culture at home. Doing this project was just the greatest thing for me because I got to express my own cultural background to the class. It made me stand out positively, creatively, alongside the roast beef and mashed potatoes the other students made out of clay. I remember my dish was colorful and exuberant with the green artichoke next to the red kidney beans, alongside the scrupulously molded grains of white rice.

That year I also made a vase with a Mayan pattern, but it was during my senior year that I truly blossomed as an artist. By senior year I was combining my art with my politics, and I gave a complete exhibition of about seven works in the Brodigan Art Gallery at Groton. Another student described my work as "an explosion of art." That was true because I felt, during my senior year, that at any moment I might indeed explode. By then my anger had become so repressed that I poured myself into sculpture and produced an exhibition of politicized art.

Some of the faculty members appreciated it, but some of the students were less tactful about expressing their views. I can still remember walking down the stairs of the dining hall, expecting to make my daily self-congratulatory rounds at the art gallery. Instead I was greeted by closed doors and my art teacher standing in front of them, arms folded. She had been waiting for me, waiting to tell me that some unknown person had vandalized the exhibit. No explanations were necessary; it was to be expected. My art had the qualities of a time bomb; it was just waiting to explode either in my own hands or in the hands of the school.

In the process of messing around with my sculpture, it appeared that someone had broken two little figures in a clay house I had constructed after the image of my own bedroom at home. The piece was titled "Save Your Soul," and I had intended to dramatize the issue of my divided consciousness at Groton. The two broken clay figures were doubles. One was seated facing the room, my bedroom, and the mirror in the room; the other was seated behind that one, looking out of the room at the viewer, facing Groton. Both of them were broken by an anonymous assailant who not only defaced my art, my two doubles, but also defaced me, the person behind the art. The symbolism was perfect! My assailant was really my accomplice; whoever broke the clay figures completed the work of art.

That little bedroom I constructed to represent me, to represent my home, contained the same picture of Jesus Christ I had tucked underneath my pillow for so many nights. The room held objects that I had to give up in order to share them with the school, to educate it about my culture as they had educated me about theirs through the community and curriculum of Groton. But in fact our relationship was not one of sharing; it was a form of cultural warfare in which my identity was to be digested by theirs. My sacrifice was symbolically completed only when the two clay figures came crashing down to represent me at Groton, to show the dissolution of my past, my culture, my own identity. Since then, I have often thought to myself that I've become the pieces of my clay figures, pieces never to be glued together quite the same way they were before I left home.

❖ ❖ ❖

GRACE KELLY, INTERPRETED
REBECA SANANDRÉS

The dress designer Rebeca SanAndrés is originally from Colombia. Now living and working in New York City, her elegant clothing for women is internationally recognized. The design pictured here is described by Rebeca as a "Grace Kelly charmeuse in silk crossed over lace with circular skirt in silk chiffon."

❇ ❇ ❇

MURALIST INCANTATION

CARLOS CUMPIÁN

Carlos Cumpián hails from San Antonio, Texas. He now lives in Chicago where he coordinates MARCH/Abrazo Press, the Nezahualcoyotl Poetry Festival, and the "La Palabra" poetry and music series.

Summer ricans gathered into
former littered lot,
where waves of concerns are
burned away, no more trash
to see, no bent splintered
floors, rotting doors to
feel a whole lot better with
our youth in view.
Hanging out the banner of
our smiles made of warmth,
aquí, on these once
glass-smashed sidewalks,
we worked hard
con multi-colored hands,
dabbin' strokin'; half-naked

we take out
our passions for slappin'
la conga and get you into
this minor masterpiece,
'cause we want the magic
of our African/Spanish/Taino
destinos to mix
mambo y salsa realities,
we can dance today
under our island and mainland
star before the weather
does a broken-treaty number
on us all, and change what
strength we painted
on this wall—
charged with the juice of
neon-soaked streets.

THERAPY IV

RICARDO ESTANISLAO ZULUETA

After their departure from Cuba in 1962, Ricardo Zulueta and his family settled in Miami, where he spent his childhood and adolescence. In 1985 he moved to New York City to complete graduate studies at New York University, having already studied art and photography at Florida International University. Lucy Lippard in her essay "Up from Under" says: "Welcome to the dark and hopeless world of Ricardo Estanislao Zulueta, which, in its very darkness and hopelessness, sheds light into the future." She quotes him as remembering that as a child in Miami "I was very secretive and formulated a secret language, and would leave notes and letters to myself in secret places." The theme of secrecy and relevation is evident in much of his work.

THERAPY IV

■ ■ ■

LABYRINTHS
ELIAS ZACKLIN

Elias Zacklin, whose maternal ancestry is Venezuelan, is a graphic artist, poet, and musician. He lives in Albuquerque, New Mexico.

LABYRINTHS

Here I am in the mist
Can't remember how to crawl
Back to my beginnings
Deep inside the Labyrinth
Murky waters sound like voices

Feel the warmth from the sands
Smell the oil on your skin
A comforting time and motion
Can hear the rhythm
Of my mother talking
Those days have passed on

23 years later
All I can capture in the mirrors
Mother and Father
How beautiful you are
Deep inside the Labyrinth
The light penetrates me
Water singing . . . guitar strings

❈ ❈ ❈

LA LLORONA

JAIME HERNANDEZ

Jaime Hernandez was born in 1959 in Oxnard, California, just north of Los Angeles. When he was old enough to hold a pencil, he began to draw cartoons. His mother, who had been an avid comic book reader all of her life, and his older brothers, Mario and Gilbert, encouraged him to draw cartoons. Television, wrestling, rock and roll music, science fiction movies and early Marvel *comics influenced his artistry. But it wasn't until the late 1970s that he seriously turned to the graphic novel art form and collaborated with his brothers Mario and Gilbert on* Love *and* Rockets, *which they initially self-published. Having performed in a rock band called Nature Boy with his brother Gilbert and his sister-in-law Carol, it's not surprising that this illustration captures a certain punk rock energy so well. "La Llorona" is the name of a band in his cartoon stories, which he notes is also the name of "a pretty famous ghost to us Mexicans."*

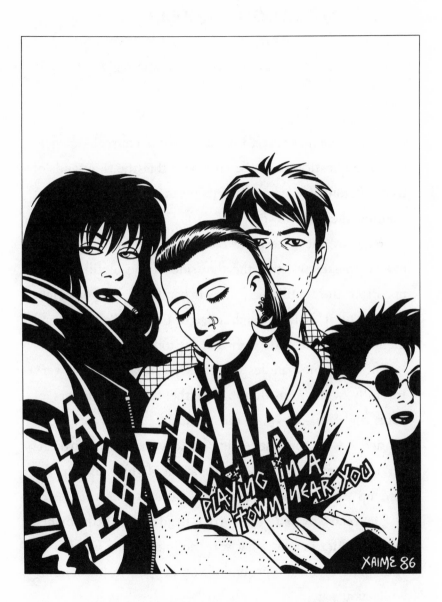

❖ ❖ ❖

TACO ETIQUETTE

REGINA CÓRDOVA

Translated from the Spanish

by Lori M. Carlson

Is there a correct way to eat a taco? Of course! But perhaps the question really is: How is it that the thousands of
taco aficionados who visit taquerías daily eat without
staining their clothes?

What are the criteria for taco etiquette? Well, first, you
have to make sure that the thin side of the tortilla is face
up. Place the tortilla in your left hand and use your right
hand to fill it. Fold the right edge of the tortilla in half and
then the opposite side over and on top of the right edge.

The way one handles a taco is essential. Hold it very
carefully with your thumb and the first two fingers of
your right hand—just the opposite if you are left-
handed—with the folded side on top. Put your third fin-
ger underneath the taco to elevate it slightly and tip the
taco up so the filling doesn't fall out.

Get ready by extending your hand just a little higher
than shoulder height. That way the juicy filling will fall on
your plate or on the ground if you happen to be standing
while you eat.

Before you take your first bite, lean forward. And enjoy! Four or five bites is all you need. If you eat your taco quickly and carefully, you will not lose a drop of the sauce. As with any activity, you have to practice, so as not to add the expense of dry cleaning to the cost of a succulent and delicious taco.

POSTAL DE MANHATITLÁN

FELIPE GALINDO-FEGGO

✠ ✠ ✠

PRAYER FOR THE MILLENNIUM
DEMETRIA MARTINEZ

Demetria Martinez has been a journalist for the
National Catholic Reporter *and the* Albuquerque
Journal. *She is the author of* Mother Tongue, *a novel,*
and Turning, *a collection of poetry. This prayer was*
inspired by a photograph by Jeffry Scott of two Central
American refugees at Southside Presbyterian Church in
Tucson, Arizona. In the early 1980s, Southside became
the first church in the nation that declared itself a safe
haven for those fleeing from starvation, strife, and
political persecution.

In our veins runs the blood of the American Indian, the
European, the African, and more. We dream of a world
where all peoples form one body, one spirit, where peace
is more beloved than war.

Corn, squash, beans, chile. We gratefully recall the foods
that have sustained us through all time. We imagine a
world where all Earth's gifts will be justly distributed.

Yerba buena, ajenjibre, manzanilla, oshá. We recall the names of *remedios* our ancestors used to heal, nourish, and renew. May we fuse together this ancient wisdom with new insights into healing. We seek wholeness, remembering that body and spirit are one. We seek justice for the poor, for without food and a home there can be no healing.

We honor the elements that allow us to live. Earth, air, water, fire. Our forebears understood that when we are out of harmony with the Earth, illness follows. We have destroyed one another and injured the Earth with weapons of war and monuments to waste. Show us the way of renewal. We can no longer say we love the Creator while destroying creation. We dream of a world envisioned in the Navajo prayer in which "All things around me are restored in beauty."

Padre Nuestro, Great Spirit, Guadalupe, Tonántzin: Our ancestors the world over knew you by many names, and spoke of you in many tongues. We respectfully acknowledge all the names of the Creator. Our indigenous forebears were called "heathen" and threatened with extinction. Our Jewish ancestors in Spain were called "heathen" and expelled from their land. Honoring all peoples who have suffered for their visions of the Creator, we dream of a world where all the names of the sacred are celebrated, and justice and peace reign.

North, South, East, West. Our ancestors moved through the Americas centuries before nations put up fences. Today, more and more people cry out for higher and stronger walls. May we have the grace to see through the walls to the faces of our *"familia."* The Mexican mother struggling to feed her family, the Central American refugee fleeing political persecution. We dream of a world where no one will be driven from home because of hunger or disaster or tyranny.

Having prayed, we set out to answer these prayers. Use our hands, our feet, our voices to re-create the world. As long as one person needlessly suffers, we all suffer. And where justice breaks through, all people move closer to a healed world. We pray, we give praise. Let the world around us be restored in beauty.

U.S. Mexico Border, Nogales, Arizona

© 1994 Jeffry D. Scott

NOTES

José Luis Ortiz, born in Mexico City, has re-
sided in New York City since 1978, where he
currently teaches at the School of Visual Arts.

PAGE 6. *El Descubrimiento de la gran Manhatitlán:*
The Discovery of Great Manhatitlán

PAGE 45. *Verano:* Summer

PAGE 51. *Hijo de la Malinche: Son of Malinche*

¡América!: America!
Yo soy americano: I am American
tengame en tu corazón: have me in your heart
como un hijo de la Malinche: like a son of
Malinche
La historia de mi raza: The history of my
people

Nunca nos desparecimos: We have never disappeared

de nuestra tierra: from our land

sino nuestra tierra: but our land

se desapareció de nosotros: disappeared from us

Somos americanos: We are Americans

PAGE 73. **DANCING FOR JOY**

Arroró mi vida	*Arroró* my life
arroró mi amor	*arroró** my love
que se duerme el niño	let my beloved child sleep
de mi corazón	

PAGE 113. *Postal de Manhatitlán:* Little Manhattan Postcard

*Arroró is the sound a small baby makes, something like goo-goo. There is no formal equivalent in English.

Acknowledgments

In my position as director of literature at the Americas Society, a few years back, I was fortunate to have met and befriended wonderful artists and writers, as well as leading thinkers and statesmen from throughout the Americas. A few have entered the pages of *Barrio Streets* as contributors and others have entered by way of inspiration and friendship. Among those I wish to acknowledge in the latter group are Ambassador George Landau, whose leadership and politesse I will always admire, and Dolores Moyano Martin, at the Library of Congress, whose scholarship and lively spirit are known so well to friends on both continents. In addition, I would like to thank Mary LeCroy at the American Museum of Natural History and Nélida Pérez and Pedro Juan at the Center for Puerto Rican Studies at Hunter College for their help and guidance pertaining to Louis Agassiz Fuertes and Pura Belpré, respectively. My mother and father are always in my thoughts as I go about my work, for it is they who gave me a strong, nurturing foundation upon which to grow both professionally and personally. And I thank Oscar Hijuelos for reasons close to the heart. Muchísimas gracias, también, to Marc Aronson, my wise editor; his assistant, Matt Rosen; and Renée Cho, my agent.

121

INDEX